Skippy Scallop

HAPPY READING!
This book is especially for:

_____

Suzanne Tate,
Author—
brings fun and
facts to us in her
Nature Series.

James Melvin,
Illustrator—
brings joyous life
to Suzanne Tate's
characters.

Suzanne and James in costume

Skippy Scallop
A Tale of Bright Blue Eyes

Suzanne Tate

Illustrated by James Melvin

Nags Head Art
Number 26 of SUZANNE TATE'S NATURE SERIES

To Donovan
whose wealth was people

Library of Congress Control Number 2003111674
ISBN 978-1-878405-43-2
ISBN 1-878405-43-8
Published by
Nags Head Art, Inc., P.O. Box 2149, Manteo, NC 27954
Copyright © 2003 by Nags Head Art, Inc.

All Rights Reserved
Printed in the United States of America

Skippy Scallop was teeny-tiny!

He was just a little egg floating free in the sea.

The water was cloudy from so many drifting eggs. There were millions of baby scallops!

But hungry sea animals would eat almost every one of them.

Skippy Scallop was scared!
And there was nothing he could do
but drift in the water.

"What can I do to be safe?" he cried one day.
He hoped someone would be listening!

A crusty old scallop, Big Blue Eyes, was the only one who heard him.

He was a big bivalve with many bright blue eyes showing between his two shells.

"Quick!" Big Blue Eyes warned.
"Here come Crabby and Nabby!"

"Climb up on a tall blade of grass.
The crabs won't find you there."

Skippy Scallop scurried up a blade of eelgrass. He hung on tightly to his new home with a special thread.

"How long will I need to stay here? Will I someday have bright blue eyes like you?" Skippy asked Big Blue Eyes.

"When you are a little older, you can drop down to the bottom," Big Blue Eyes replied. "Then, you can clap your shells together and skip away."

"Soon, you will have many blue eyes like mine.
We can see only shadows. But our eyes will always warn of moving things that might hurt us."

Big Blue Eyes had lived only two years
— but that's old for a scallop!
He had escaped from many a sea star and crab.

The old scallop looked like he had been around for a long time!
His upper shell was covered with tiny plants and animals growing on it.

Big Blue Eyes could easily hide with all that on top of his shell!

And those tiny animals had a free ride to food everyday — wherever the scallop went.

Crabby and Nabby could hurt even
an old scallop like Big Blue Eyes.
He didn't like to be around them.

"I'm leaving now!" he said. Big Blue Eyes quickly clapped
his shells together and shot out jets of water.
Then, he slipped and slid backwards!

Skippy Scallop watched Big Blue Eyes jet away and wished that he could be bigger and older.

But he slurped plankton — tiny plants and animals — and stayed on that blade of grass.

Before long, he was big enough to drop down to the bottom. His two little shells had grown larger, and there were bright blue eyes between them!

Danger was everywhere for a young scallop.
But Skippy could do two things:

1. Close his shells quickly whenever
an enemy was near or

2. clap his shells together
and skip away!

Skippy soon grew larger from eating plenty of plankton.
He found other scallops and began to live with them.

The scallops rested in the bottom while they ate.
They didn't burrow like their cousins, the clams.

One day, while he was feeding, Skippy's new blue eyes warned him:

LOOK OUT FOR

And sure enough, an animal that would like
to eat Skippy was moving toward him!
It was Spiny Sea Star.

Skippy was scared!
Quickly, he clapped his shells together
and skipped away — backwards!

Skippy moved so fast that sand kicked up in the water.
It helped to hide the young scallop,
and Spiny Sea Star couldn't find him.

Skippy Scallop skipped for joy!
He was safe one more time.

But he skipped right by the den of another scary animal — Oozey Octopus! There were shells from many meals in front of his den.

Big Blue Eyes appeared again beside Skippy. "Quick! Move away from there!" he warned. "Look at all those shells from scallops that didn't escape from Oozey Octopus."

Skippy listened to Big Blue Eyes and quickly skipped away from Oozey's den.

Then, Skippy's blue eyes warned him that strange big animals were swimming close to him!

But Big Blue Eyes told Skippy,
"You don't need to be afraid this time."

"Those are HELPFUL HUMANS," he said. "I've seen them before — they have come to the bay to see how many scallops they can count."

"HELPFUL HUMANS hope that we are healthy. They know that scallops can't live here unless the water is clean."

"I'm glad that HUMANS care about us," Skippy said. Then, he clapped his shells together and happily skipped away!